W9-CIB-387

NICKI WEISS

Where Does the Brown Bear Go?

GREENWILLOW BOOKS, New York

Library of Congress Cataloging-in-Publication Data

Weiss, Nicki.
Where does the brown bear go?/ by Nicki Weiss.
p. cm.
Summary: When the lights go down on the city street and the sun sinks far behind the seas, the animals of the world are on their way home for the night.
ISBN 0-688-07862-1. ISBN 0-688-07863-X (lib. bdg.)
[1. Animals—Fiction. 2. Night—Fiction.]
I. Title. PZ7.W448145Wh 1989
[E]—dc19 87-36980 CIP AC

Colored pencils were used for the full-color art.
The text type is Weidemann Medium.

Printed in Hong Kong by South China Printing Co. First Edition 10 9 8 7 6 5 4 3

FOR JOHNNY

AND STEVIE

When the lights go down
On the city street,
Where does the white cat go, honey?
Where does the white cat go?

Bakery
THES

When evening settles
On the jungle heat,
Where does the monkey go, honey?
Where does the monkey go?

They are on their way.

They are on their way home.

When shadows fall
Across the dune,
Where does the camel go, honey?
Where does the camel go?

When the junkyard is lit
By the light of the moon,
Where does the stray dog go, honey?
Where does the stray dog go?

They are on their way.

They are on their way home.

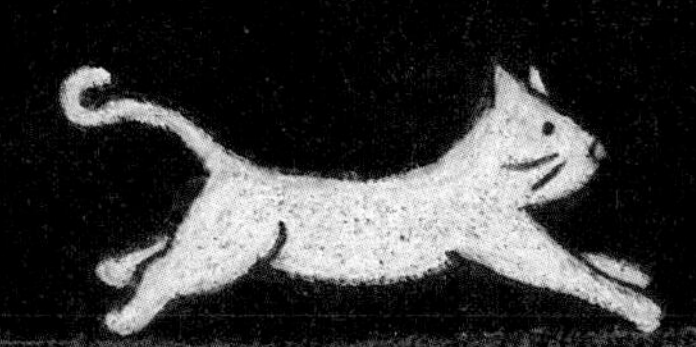

When the sun sinks far
Behind the seas,
Where does the seagull go, honey?
Where does the seagull go?

When night in the forest
Disguises the trees,
Where does the brown bear go, honey?
Where does the brown bear go?

They are on their way.

They are on their way home.

The stars are bright and a warm wind blows
Through the window tonight, honey,
Through the window tonight....

And everyone is home.